To all my grandchildren

'S LAST VOYAGE

by
EDWARD ARDIZZONE

Henry Z. Walck, Inc.

Library of Congress Cataloging in Publication Data

Ardizzone, Edward, date.
  Tim's last voyage.

  SUMMARY: Tim and Ginger run into
trouble when they sail as deck hands
on the Arabella.

[1. Sea stories] I. Title.
PZ7.A682Tis   [E]   72-10112
ISBN 0-8098-1200-2

ISBN: 0-8098-1200-2
Library of Congress Catalog Card Number: 72-10112
Printed in the United States of America

A gale was blowing. It was night. Tim, who lived
in a house by the sea, could hear the waves crash-
ing on the beach. He could not sleep. He loved
the sea and longed to be in some small ship
battling with the storm.

The next morning Tim and his friends Ginger and Charlotte walked down to the beach. The gale was blowing harder than ever. The waves were enormous and the three of them had lots of fun racing the waves as they rushed up the shingle beach.

Sometimes Ginger was foolish and would nearly get caught.

Then they climbed the steep shingle bank to talk to the old boatman.

'It is bad, bad!' said the boatman. 'See that line of white foam far out to sea? That is where even bigger waves are breaking in the shallow water of the Goodwin Sands. I will bet my bottom dollar there will be some poor ship

wrecked on those treacherous sands before the
month is out.'

'Oh poof!' said Ginger. 'I've seen worse
storms than this.'

After leaving the boatman they walked to the harbour nearby.

There, lying beside the quay, was a small steamer with a tall rusty red funnel. It was called the S.S. *Arabella*.

What a lovely name, thought Tim, saying 'Arabella, Arabella' over and over again to himself.

Hanging on the side of the ship was a notice on which was written 'WANTED DECK HANDS for short VOYAGE 3 DAYS ONLY.'

'Oh!' said Tim. 'How I wish we could get that job, but my father and mother would not like it.'

But Ginger only answered 'Poof! It's holiday time. The job is only for three days. They won't mind.'

Then they all climbed on board and met the mate who told them that as the ship was due to sail soon and as no men had applied for the job he would give it to Tim and Ginger. But he warned them that the work was hard and that the bosun was a tartar.

Tim told Charlotte to run home and tell his parents that he and Ginger would be away for three days. Then they went below to find the bosun and learn what jobs they had to do.

The bosun was indeed a tartar. 'What! Two snippets like you?' he shouted. 'I will work your fingers to the bone. See the carpenter, get pails and scrubbing brushes and, if I catch either of you idling, I will beat him with a rope's end.'

Joey Adze the ship's carpenter, handyman and storesman looked at them over his spectacles. 'Well! Well! Well! You are pretty small aren't

you!' he said. 'Here are brushes, pails and mops. Do the best you can and avoid the bosun, he's a TARTAR.'

Tim and Ginger were hard at work scrubbing out the saloon when the *Arabella* left port. At once she felt the force of the gale and rolled and pitched, which made Tim and Ginger's work harder still.

The bosun never allowed them to rest so they were two very tired little boys when they handed back their pails and brushes to Joey.

'You do look tired,' said Joey. 'I can see that the bosun has been a TARTAR as usual. Come dry your eyes, Ginger, and both of you make yourselves as comfortable as possible and rest.'

After they had rested for a little, Joey asked if either of them could read. When Tim said yes he gave him a book and said 'Read it to me.' The book was called *Moby Dick*. It was about a white whale.

'I was a whaler once,' said Joey. 'I have seen a white whale. It was a brute.'

Because it was so rough the *Arabella* could not get into the small port which was its destination. Instead it steamed south into the gale.

These were hard days; for the Captain who could not leave the bridge; for the mate who had to see that everything was shipshape; for Gino the cook because it was difficult to cook in rough weather; for Joey patching and mending; and for Tim and Ginger because the bosun with his rope's end made them work all day long, not caring if they were cold, wet and tired.

On the fourth day out a terrible thing happened.
A great wave dashed over the side and washed the
funnel overboard.

Water poured into the engine room. The engines stopped and the *Arabella* rolled like a dead thing in a waste of waters.

McAndrew the engineer came up from below saying that he could not start the engine again but would do his best.

The bosun, when he heard the news, cried out 'It's a doomed ship!' and shut himself in his cabin with a bottle of rum. You see he was a coward as well as a bully.

Ginger was frightened and sat huddled in a corner of the galley. Gino tried to cheer him up with tit bits of food.

For what seemed many days the helpless ship was blown to the north by the gale.

The Captain was worried because, as he could not see the sun by day nor the stars by night, he did not know where they were.

The mate was worried because there was three foot of water in the hold and still more coming on board.

The engineer was worried because he could not get the engines to start nor the pumps to work.

Gino was worried because he could not cook hot food for the crew and poor Ginger could not be comforted. But Ginger did try hard not to be so frightened and to help Gino cut bread and cheese.

The bosun only howled and shouted 'It's a doomed ship!' and drank more rum. This upset other members of the crew when they heard him.

All this time Tim and Joey sat stitching a great sail to go on the foremast and help steady the ship. When Tim's fingers became too sore to go

on stitching he would wedge himself into a corner and read *Moby Dick* to Joey. This made them both feel happier.

At last the sail was finished and with the help of the mate and some of the crew they ran it up the foremast. The wind filled it, the ship was steadier and less water came on board.

But, all the same, the gale drove them north-ward even faster than before and the Captain was

even more worried because he still
did not know where they were.

On to the north they went until one day there was a grinding crash. The poor *Arabella* bounced and shuddered to a stop. She had run aground

and was at the mercy of the breaking waves which dashed over her and carried away her boats and ventilators.

The Captain was very brave and very calm. He called the crew on deck. 'Men,' he said, 'this looks like the end of my dear ship *Arabella* and

it might be the end of us too. In a sea like this the ship will break up soon. Our boats are gone. Collect all the wood you can and make rafts so you can float ashore. But I do wish I knew where we were.'

At that moment there was a rift in the clouds
and the sun shone through. Tim saw a distant
beach and a house behind it. It was his house.
'Sir,' he shouted to the Captain, 'I can see my

house. We must be on the Goodwin Sands. The old boatman is sure to see us and tell the life-boatmen.' 'Good, but they must hurry,' answered the Captain, 'as we are sinking fast.'

Tim was right. The old boatman had seen them and told the lifeboatmen. The lifeboat, a grand new one with an engine, arrived just in time to save them all before the *Arabella* sank beneath the boiling foam.

Even now, if the weather is fine and the tide is low and you are standing on Tim's shingle beach looking far out to sea, you will make out two masts sticking up above the shallow waters of those treacherous sands. They are the *Arabella*'s.

Once in the lifeboat the bosun felt safe and became his old bullying self again. He said he would beat the boys with his rope's end if they would not sit still.

As for Ginger, when somebody said 'You

were frightened, weren't you?', he answered 'Poof! I was very brave helping Gino in the galley.' Gino said that Ginger had tried hard not to be frightened and was quite a help, which pleased Tim a lot.

Standing on the beach to watch the arrival of the lifeboat were Tim's father and mother and Charlotte. They were very surprised to see Tim and Ginger as they had no idea that the wrecked ship was the *Arabella*. They gave them a great welcome.

When all the hugging and kissing was over, Tim's mother made him promise not to go to sea again until he was grown up. Tim kept his promise.

But, when he was quite grown up he did go to sea and in time became a very fine sailor and the Captain of a great ship.

However he always remembered the time when he had been a little boy in a ship, so he was never unkind to his cabin boys and never beat them with a rope's end.